# Yip and Yap

by Susan Hartley • illustrated by Anita DuFalla

The pup can run at Kit.

"Yip, yap," said the pup.

"No, pup!" said Pop.

"Do not yip and yap now!"

"Pop, do not yell
at the pup," said Jen.
"The pup is not big yet."

"Yip, yip, yap," said
the pup. "Yap, yap, yip."
Pam said, "No, pup!
I want a nap now."

4

Jen said, "Pam, do not yell at the pup. He is not big yet."

The pup said, "Yip, yip, yip!"
"I do not like this," said Bob.
"Pam, Pop, and I
do not like this!"
"Yap, yap," said the pup.

"No, pup!" said Jen.
"Pam, Bob, and Pop
do not like this!
I do not like this!"

"Yes!" said Jen.
"Kit can do this!
Now the pup will
not yip and yap."